DOG GONE

DOG GONE

Coping With The Loss of a Pet
HOWARD BRONSON

A BESTSELL BOOK

6 Samba Circle
Sandwich, MA 02563

Permission should be addressed in writing to: Bestsell Publications
6 Samba Circle, Sandwich, MA 02563.

Library of Congress Cataloging-in-Publication Data

Bronson, Howard F., 1953-
Dog Gone
1. Consolation, Pet 2. Bronson, Howard F., 1953-
3. Bronson, Grady I. Title
ISBN 0-9616807-8-4   93-072871

Printed in the United States of America

Editors

Philosophical/Ethical Continuity: Harriet Kreitzer
Proofreader : Nyles Freedman Editing Services

Cover Design & Illustration: Skip Morrow

Pre-press, including page design, art placement,
layout and pasteup: Todd Souza, New Wave Printing, Falmouth, Massachusetts

Special Acknowledgement

A few months before press-time, we had a problem: while the book was finished and testing well, it still needed something more. Then one day, my young daughter declared that she would create 'drawings for the doggie book.' Since we felt that this book was geared more for adults, we delicately downplayed the idea at first.

Then it sank in, like when a dog finally responds to its name for the first time. Heartfelt pictures from children was exactly what this book needed, so we held a contest at the local primary school, hoping to get a few responses from which we would choose ten for the book.

Much to our overwhelming surprise, we received hundreds of wonderful responses from talented children from kindergarten through eighth grade. All the pictures were beautiful and special and we wish we had the room to put them all in. In fact, instead of ten pictures, we choose over fifty.

So to every single child at the Oak Ridge School in beautiful Sandwich, Massachusetts who participated in our contest: the love of your pets shines through in your work. Thanks to your work, <u>Dog Gone </u>is now complete.

Contents

Dedication

To the slaughtered elephant,
the disemboweled goat..
to the mink & her loved ones
who made up a coat.

To the dolphin, the snail, the rhesus macax,
to the helpless that fall,
with the fall of the axe.

To the great mother whale
and burrows we find fox in.

To their daily demise
by the deluge of toxin.

To all of God's creatures
so helpless to greed,
to the blood that man lusts for
when there's none left to bleed.

"Mr. Mustache" by Rebecca Shakin Age 11

Introduction

As if with toothy smile, wagging tail, and a tongue too big for the mouth, I welcome you and invite you to sit back and get comfortable as I relate the true story of the strangest dog you could ever hope to meet. A dog with human eyes and a soul of endless dimension; a dog full of unyielding love, support and control of all he encountered. A pet not unlike your pet. A dumb dog; a brilliant entity; an amazing creature bound in wisdom as deep and endless as his sheepdog fur.

Grady; what a guy you were and what a pure definition of a friend you will always be.

Maybe he wasn't so strange after all; no stranger than the pet that may have touched your life at some point. We miss and love those who loved and honored us and that's good, happy, sad. That's everything.

So turn off the TV for an hour, cuddle up with your beloved and come celebrate that amazing phenomenon we call pet . You'll see your own animal somewhere in these pages and you'll wonder something quite profound like, 'who's really crazy here?'

Enjoy.

"Mountain"
by Madeline Powers
Age 6

I do believe every human's secret desire is to be
a child forever...and to grow up?
Never!

I miss him and I should be content, grateful to have known
this playful pulverizer of bone,

and I should accept that by coming together, we
are now forever never
alone.

One last hug...

I could have used one last fuzzy smelly hug

to stare into those soulful eyes
to know we are forever connected.

Our time with you meant everything to you
and your love meant everything to us and
now that your brief visit to our home is over and done,
I am not relieved that your suffering in your old age is
over.

You were my walking companion
after a long day of writing my books,
you loved me when no one else could.
You always understood and now that you're gone...
the one private safe harbor
of uncompromising love in my life...
isn't there.
And I am frightened by the discomfort.

Why don't we ever get those last hugs like in the movies?
Why don't we get to say...goodbye?

"Mickey Mantle" by Joanna Teixeira Age 9

"Don't Forget Me"

How quickly life eases us back from whence we came as that special omnipresence of that special pet shockingly becomes just the memory of a lovely and wonderful visitor.

In a nursing home, the other day, as I peered curiously into the rooms, one of the doorways revealed a quivering old man, quite emaciated, obviously ill; his taut skin, far too excessive for his delicate body, his breathing labored. Yet, his face bore a great calm and his half-closed eyes suggested only a sense of tranquility, and a life thoroughly lived. As with so many who curl up for that final rest, his fetal-position was not unusual and actually produced an air of comfort, peace. Readiness.

It reminded me of the first time we ever lay eyes upon Grady who was in his favorite self-cuddling position; plopped down like a wad of mud yet graced by the position of his head which he draped over the top of his front right leg. That first time we saw him was the day he was supposed to be put to sleep, as we humans so artfully put it.

We hadn't even planned upon ever seeing an animal in such sorry shape. We had been shopping for a bright, shiny new puppy to adopt and bond with. How did we end up at this place catching accidental glances at this pathetic and bludgeoned rag of an animal?

But the urgency in the volunteer's voice who called us, the one who was supposed to call us with information

By Stephen Hickey Age 7

about new puppies, prompted us to climb in our car one hot and smoggy Saturday morning and head for the L.A. County pound. She told us that she knew nothing about this dog except that it was a purebred Old English. And that this was its tenth day, the day it would be put to sleep if no one lay claim. No stays, no extensions, no reprieve from the governor.

Down we headed toward the dusty heart of central L.A., following detailed directions to an area we never knew existed. Down further and deeper into an ever-thickening smoggy abyss, as if crossing through a bleak time-threshold, until the haze cleared somewhat to reveal a series of windowless stucco buildings, painted that awful off-green, the one you wonder why paint companies ever manufactured in the first place.

Dog-pounds make a statement about the absolute best and worst of who we are. Because of overcrowded cages and limited staff, there were some volunteers making the effort not just to feed the dogs but also to try to give them some reassurance, knowing full-well that most of these animals would never go home again. Some came here because they were lost; others arrived, hungry, dog-tags cut, obviously abandoned. Some were brought here because their owners could no longer care for them. Some were unwanted puppies because someone still didn't get the message about spaying or neutering.

As we walked from our car past one of the stark, windowless structures and entered through a tall, chain-link gate, I was saddened to see so many beautiful animals just laying in cages. I was struck by a dulling sense of

3

finality, as if in a 'Doggie Auschwitz' and tried without success to resist the strong sense that very few four-legged prisoners, no matter how innocent, would ever get out alive. To this day, I do not understand why more potential pet-owners don't have the sense to visit a dog-pound first so we might save more innocent animals.

As hard as I tried to be cold, the accidental glances at so many helpless eyes captured my heart, as if asking ,"why this final punishment?"

Past the sea of dark, begging eyes through the cages, beyond more mysterious windowless buildings, some with ominous aluminum smokestacks, then down a long gravel path to a hidden corner adjacent to the most uncomfortably-smelling building; here was a gaunt gathering of dogs somehow more sorry-looking than the rest. It was obvious that this was 'death-row'; obvious to us and to the animals.

Unlike the others elsewhere in the pound still in possession of sufficient spirits to at least recant the best of their former lives with the wag of a tail and a doggie-smile, these doomed souls seemed to have lost their will to express even a paucity of hope. They knew their time was coming. They would not fight the doctor who would administer the Sodium Pentothal. They would die peacefully and politely and then be disposed of somewhere as ash and cinder, perhaps as part of the oozing deep-city haze that enveloped our arrival.

You could see the resignation in this heap of dogs. You could see that they had given up hope of a returning master, and that their contact with anything resulted from their hopeless sprawl on the cold, soiled cement floor of the waiting-cubicles, as the final hours crawled mercilessly by.

Lying in the midst of this heap was an ugly, battered mass of a dog already far closer to death than life. "That's him," said the volunteer who escorted us. "You want him ?"

Why we didn't turn and leave immediately, I will never be able to explain. He was shaved to the skin, bloody red scabs and splotches covered his legs and parts of his upper torso. He was so mangled, so obviously sick, he couldn't even get up and walk to the side of his cage to greet his potential saviors. This was an Old English Sheepdog?

Yet, in that head-over-leg position, he was somehow well, it may best be explained by observing that no decent human can resist an animal that is either excessively cute, or excessively hopeless. What an amazing phenomenon to observe that as an animal loses all ability to appeal, in its deterioration, it can elicit the greatest degree of come-hitherness and grace, like the dying old man. It certainly worked on us as we found our mouths speaking "okay, we'll take him" as if prompted by some outside force.

We signed the adoption papers, paid the five-dollar fee, made an additional donation and then this pathetic creature was ours. What made us do this? We mostly carried this dying animal to our sparkling, clean new car, lifted him into the back seat where his legs immediately gave way causing him to splay out like an old rag.

As I put the key in the ignition, I felt this dry, scratchy, quivering tongue bearing down on my ear; a thank-you kiss from our new adopted pet. It was the very moment we knew we had done the right thing.

In the years that followed as Grady blossomed into one of the most beautiful of sheepdogs and finest of companions, we were constantly rewarded for snatching this once-helpless creature from the fingertips of Hell.

By Ginger Lennon Age 9

I thought of this story recently because of how Grady died. He left us strong, loved and loving, curled up in that same position as we first saw him many years back. Head draped over that front right leg, in the tranquility of sleep, he dreamt his final paw-quivering dreams, and then forever jumped and bounced into our dreams.

At the Pine Ridge Cemetery for Small Animals in Dedham, Massachusetts, we buried Grady after a simple service. The fee again was five-dollars.

"Grady" by Ashley Bronson Age 8

How quickly life eases us back
from whence we came

and how life will never-ever be the same...

so don't forget me,
the old dog cries

with a faint whimper and tears of joy.

Don't forget me,
I protected you
when you were a little boy.

By Sean McDonough Age 6

Par*tick*ularly Testy

No halcyonic, bird-chirping summer near any wetland area is complete without that early season ritual of removing those little lightly hued marble-shaped things with all those legs sticking out, from the family dog.

As far as I can see, ticks do have one positive reason for being; they have frightened a goodly number of fair-weather, Lyme-Disease-paranoid friends away. Other than that, their link in the intricate weave of life has not one single thread of purpose.

Why did they torture my poor dog! As he innocently pranced through woods and tall grass earnestly carrying out whatever urgent mission he felt compelled to accomplish, these dispassionate freeloaders would hitch rides and burrow deep within his sea of fur.

Here is where Grady became their last supper. They would plug into his body and sup on his blood as if it were an endless chocolate float. Like a cartoon-character, they would eat nonstop becoming within just a few hours, a round bloated mass, many times their original size.

These characters never walk away from this diner. Ticks eat...until they explode. Not a great life.

For hundreds of millions of years, this odd exploding species has endured, which can only mean that they must be doing something right. God only knows what.

Our job of course was to interrupt these meals as early as possible: 1) to reduce the possibility of infection and 2) to allow Grady to retain some of his own blood for his own personal use.

And as gentle a soul as my dog was, and he was among the gentlest, and as highly skilled as we became at *tickus mealus interruptus*, we could not remove some ticks without an angry bite from a suddenly pinched pooch.

"Hey, watch it," is what he'd be saying in teethy, snarling dog-speak. We'd apologize with soothing voice and gentle hands, then would continue on at our ginger-best. Still, there were par*tick*ular zones which would momentarily transform this otherwise angelic creature into the *Dog-i-nator*.

I don't know how to cite the following example without offending the sensibilities of many of my readers so please accept my apologies in advance. I'll be as general as words permit.

For some reason, the ticks' favorite diner was located right around Grady's backside which abutted some of his most restricted real estate. No big surprise there but certainly a major problem for the well-meaning tick eviction squad.

How do you remove a tick from a particularly sensitive zone, from an animal whose response will be to hunt you down as priority kibble? Read on and become enlightened.

"Browny" by Paige Titus Age 7

First we'd roll him on his back, legs akimbo, tick-site exposed. One of us would hold his head calm and still. The other surgeon, tweezers-a-blazin', would circle and site the target, then begin counting slowly...One...Beads of sweat building...Two.."hold his head" "ready tweezers?" "Will we mess up? Will we die? Will this be the last thing we ever do?"

"Three!" Within less than a tenth of a second, the tweezers have gripped the beast and pulled, then both surgeons run in opposite directions as fast and as far as they can. Our suddenly tickless dog, now quite ticked-off, doesn't know who to kill first but by the time he rolls over, jaws snapping, the surgeons are practicing in the next county.

Many minutes later (which is like a season to a dog) all was forgotten and for the moment our sheepdog was himself again and the world's most dangerous diner, was closed.

All that was left was a happy dog, a peaceful summer afternoon and a few gawking neighbors wondering how we knew the tick was there in the first place.

"Missy" by AnnMarie PaPasodero Age 7

"Maggie" by Alicia Persico Age 7

First World

As a child it was Duke, a rare black collie. We were in-separable, always running through warm embracing grassy fields or the oak-enshrouded brook that trickled lazily through the backyards of our perfect suburban neighborhood;   our   nothing-ever-happens-here neighborhood..quiet, ordinary, yet wrought with new daily adventures and excitement whenever Duke and I set off to explore these great domains.

Those days, like a deep breath after a nap, like a chocolate cupcake; those days, always warm with excitement. The sheer innocent pleasure of the child in all of us; unstained, hiding.

This is about innocence and peace, eons before the body grows much bigger, before the approach of the great para-dox of losing our own innocence in order to fight for the preservation of the child in our own offspring. This is all a dog knows. Duke then Grady.

Come with me. I'm going back to that place now. C'mon! It's the same as I first found it when I was three, a place of friendship, unquestioned and unconditional, an ex-tremely kind, forgiving place where no judgements are made so no reprimands need ever be given. The safest haven; an endless song in a gleeful child's heart.

All are welcome always but very few choose to come. Lot of kids live here from everywhere and of course all their pets and a few lucky adults. You can't arrive there in a fancy car. Money has no purpose. Every day is warm and cozy.

It is a place where a child and dog can bond forever. And when that dog dies, a child may not go back there sometimes for many years. Until one day a new dog comes, reawakening a rusty communication and another visit to that secret place, only to discover that it's the same as it's always been.

Grady took me back there for a while and I resent the rude thrust back to adulthood.

"Fife" by Brittany Lonergan Age 6

"Fluffy" by Sara Knippenberg Age 7

Touch

Speaking.........Words...are...

but a meager form of communication

so if you haven't learned to understand your dog,

I hope you've at least learned patience.

So give me a world of innocent joy

and I'll tell you a story of a dog and his boy..

where the simplest things

mean everything.

If you don't understand, I apologize.

I didn't mean to excite you,

I just wanted to open your eyes

because what you don't know

could bite you!

"Shaggie" by Kristin Taylor Age 9

Still Life

It hurts to know you're not around...
that fuzzy rump that bounced through town.
The kitchen table. "Go lie down!"
Your messes that our shoe-soles found

But you and your rump...were always...'round.

The ticks & fleas that hounded you,
the dish-collar you wore so you wouldn't chew.
Your stomach haunts oft changed our view,
and when unbathed, well, you stunk. P.U.!

Still it felt so good to be with you.

Your fur, it wound up everywhere
even now and it's been a year!
You'd bite us if we neared your food
(I think that was rather rude!)

Still my memories are so good.
I'm glad you graced our neighborhood.
You were our soul's constant clown
and it hurts to know you're not around.

By Michael Ashmankas Age 10

And the Raven Slept

In retrospect, Grady's death was no surprise at all. For the last month of his life, he really didn't want to take his daily saunters through the forest. "I'll just sleep through these lazy summer days, thank you."

I was a bit concerned when he ceased his ferocious welcome for any and all strangers at the door (including me, sometimes). Even the parade of young and innocent door-to-door evangelists for whom he reserved his most threatening display, broken teeth in full frothy regalia; in his final weeks, nary even a curious flip of the ear. Still we reassured ourselves that he was simply behaving like an old dog laden with the discomfort of those hot and sticky days.

Then the robins came; the robins, gone for so many years; the robins who had from afar feared the sight of this dog or even his scent. Suddenly right in front of this most terrorsome old guard, they had blanketed the property, their burnt-orange chests dotting every tree brush and gutter. The robins who had for so long lived in constant secrecy, often shielded by the intricate weave of the tall juniper bushes were also hiding from an even more dreaded specter; the ever-present and often deadly egg-robbing raven. Even with this looming terror of certain death, the robins had taken over as if no raven had ever existed.

What instilled this ever timid, ever cautious bird with such a sudden self-assuredness? This was a very unusual turn of natural events.

As a further trivial wonder (you know, the ones you don't share with anyone for fear of being institutionalized), where were the ravens? They who ruled and blackened the sky, brazenly cawing as if in deadly revenge, eliciting in the most hardened among us, a sense of something being quite wrong; always there just as the sky is at its gloomiest, as if dictated by some immeasurable force in this haunting bird's possession. This raven, this center point of our nightmares.

"Grady" by Rachel Bronson Age 7

The raven, who for years without fear or hesitation, would drop down by Grady's dinner and while selecting a few choice kibble would tauntingly eye the old dog as he began his futile pursuit. Slowly, the big bird would bounce a few steps and then lift upwards, just in time, just out of reach from Grady's snapping jaws and ravenous eyes

24

which just a moment earlier, spake a sense of certainty that this time, he would wrest this hateful prey right out of the open sky and thrash it mercilessly to the ground.

Each attempt ended as the one before, with a laughing giant black bird, and a frustrated dog's hope of a next time coupled with his very short memory.

This ever-present winged nemesis who never tired of this cruel game were for the first time, replaced by the once-most cautious of birds. The robin knew it was now safe to make our home its proud domain.

The most spectacular sight was yet to come as I awakened to find a band of robins plucking some kibble from the deadly dog dish, stretching their beaks to their utmost. These birds in particular always preferred the natural yield of the surrounding woodlands; yet here they felt drawn to show their lack of fear. Safe from a potential deadly swallow of the great hairy beast and safe from instant finish by the nonchalant grasp of the giant shimmering blackbird. Everything was different but why?

The birds knew because they could see what no human will ever see. The ravens stopped coming because the great old dog could no longer give even a mildly threatening chase and ravens will not stay around without a worthy opponent to play the game with. But what about the robins; how did they know it was safe after all these years? They knew because they could see what no medical technology will ever see. They could sense Grady's heart was marching out to its final steps and in knowing this beyond reproach, they came and feasted.

This great cycle that makes even the raven sleep, is nature's way of intertwining the old into the new so that nothing ever dies cold and alone. Even on the darkest winter day, nature provides for a marching out in perfect cadence, graceful in rhythm, cruel in its finality.

Tired and gracefully fading, Grady's time had come to hear the robin's song.

By Greg Losordo Age 9

Each creature works for one safe haven
and some by chance must pay the raven.

The plover nest, no branches reach
scatter eggs on grass-swept beach.
Humans come and eggs are crushed
Yet somehow one goes on untouched.

Life goes on without behavin'
who knows where may lurk the raven.

No old storybook classic here
as life moves souls from here to there.

So if your life for now is bad,
don't be mournful, don't be sad.

Love all good times as safe haven.
Time is short till comes the raven.

"Jake" by Nicholas James Behlman Age 8

Courage 101

Some people automatically believe that animals smell badly. Actually animals smell quite well but only in the tracking sense. Most animals depend upon their sense of smell as early radar and can smell danger long before we know what's going on. The heavy head springs up, nostrils begin flaring and pulsing like two cartoon trumpets while you sit there wondering what your pet sees or hears or smells, usually getting your answer minutes later by means of a knock at the door, a rainstorm or in some cases, never and you wonder; why the false alarm? Perhaps it's your pet's way of getting a little attention by acting important.

For years, I have prided myself as one capable of walking into the lion's den and surviving only slightly scathed, often having confidence when I had no right nor reason to. Here and now I reveal my secret; the lions could not smell fear and that has rung true for virtually all the dogs I have encountered (with the exception of course of the trained killers who don't care what you exude).

Essentially, I love dogs and pose no threat to them. They in turn pose none for me. Of course not everyone is that lucky and have seen the often horrific results of either showing fear or by simply being in the wrong place at the wrong time.

Fear conveys one specific message to a dog; that you fear harm only because you intend harm. The dog intends to be nice and loving. That's how they're born; not unlike kids. Nowadays when I strut into a major boardroom or courthouse, full of human bulldogs, waiting for me to show fear, I can often send them off shaking their heads with their tails between their legs. Often an intended enemy becomes a friend.

Grady taught me courage and that the fearsome must expend a great deal of energy to create and maintain this beast. Fear is the beast, not the animal. I only wish I had learned to listen better.

"Precious" by Greg Perkins Age 8

"Misty" by Elizabeth Boulay Age 8

All Rise

You'll notice throughout these writings that I never use the term 'dog-owner' for two very specific reasons: The first is that no one can really own a dog. You can pay money, sometimes a lot of money for a dog but you can't own the spiritual essence that makes your dog special.

The second reason is far more significant, especially for those who might still insist that they own their pets. We made that mistake. In the beginning, we assumed that we owned Grady. For many years, it was automatic. Of course we owned this dog, of course he was ours without question.

In the evenings, that was our dog who curled up with us next to the fireplace while we read or watched television, exhausted after another arduous workday.

Ahh, perfect; cozy and settled-in until Grady would suddenly get up and tap urgently at the back door. As the taps grew louder we debated as to who would break their repose to let him out "You're closer" "No, you're closer!" "Come on, honey, *please*!"

Up the loser would begrudgingly meander to the door and out would go Grady who as soon as he saw us settled back in, would insist upon being let in whether he did his business or not.

After several false alarms ("I just let him out. It's your turn to let him in"), he would finally go out and do his thing for real.

By Ashley Bronson Age 8

Up and down. Up and down and in a vigilant effort to protect our new carpet, we complied every time. All he had to do was beckon.

Then there were the rainstorms. He'd scratch at the front door desperate to egress but once he saw the rain, would halt abruptly probably thinking, "I ain't goin out there. It's raining in the front yard. " So what would he do? He'd turn around and head straight for the back yard ("maybe it's sunny back there"). After rediscovering each time that a rainstorm in the front yard also meant it was raining in the backyard, he would retreat and burrow in a corner, refusing to go out but would stare at us constantly. "This rain is your fault. Now stop it."

He wouldn't move, eat or go to the bathroom, sometimes for days until, according to him, we made it stop raining.

Then he would spring out of hibernation and out the door, all systems normal.

Are you beginning to see who owned whom? He had us well-trained and we never caught on. In fact, now that he's gone, we still get up and just walk to the door and then stop ourselves. It's reflex.

Grady, you brought so much love and happiness into our home. You made us laugh, cry and laugh and get up. A lot (and not always in time). But most of all, you made us worry!

By Caitlin Cook Age 8

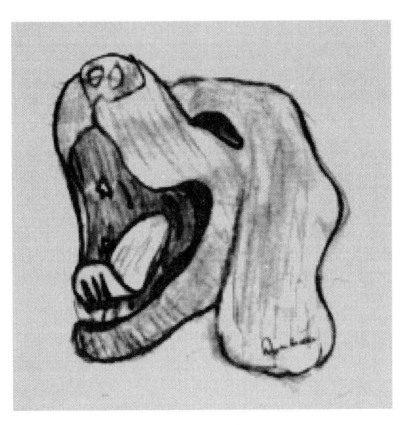

"Brandy" by Ryan Green Age 11

Killer Dogs

If people are people and dogs are dogs.. if we live like civilized people until we act like dogs, what chance does a dog have to be decent? At their best, people are the best 'people'.. At their worst, people are animals.

What a bad rap befalls the innocent healthy dog. Healthy! What about that one! When we're healthy, we're fit human beings. When we're not, we're sick as dogs.

Yet I've seen the puppy mills, those places where dogs are treated as breeding machines and kept in tiny elevated cages for their entire and very short lives. As a result their heavily distributed offspring are often malnourished, ill or deformed.

I've seen the dead rats creeping around the sludge dumped years ago by the nearby air-base; dead rats who are often eaten by the progressive food-chain resulting in dead turtles, foxes, mice, birds and deer.

I've seen the baby seals crying helplessly as they are battered to death and the dolphin's last cackle as it suffocates in the massive commercial fish nets. Same with the sea turtle, whose scratchy hiss, when trapped in a similar setting, is barely audible.

And the most haunting of all audibles; the silence, as when another unnecessary development gets pushed through and suddenly where birds and once squirrels thrived is now dust and stone. The habitat is not remade elsewhere. The species diminishes.

"Shiloh" by Kirsten Lawson Age 9

Humankind sells us hope to counter our fears; glitzy promises that all will be better, that we will turn things around, the cruelty will cease and the animals will come back. Yet I've seen the woods year after year and with each new year, I see fewer animals.

Is this the best of man? Is this who we really are? I've complained about this a lot but have been told my bark is worse than my bite.

By Ashley Bronson Age 8

Ouch

Ahh, to be young and in love. Ahh, to be old and in love;...that's even better.

Our dog had given so much love to the family. Why shouldn't he have a love of his own? So we made our diligent efforts to help him sniff out a nice lady to settle down with.

We made several attempts to introduce Grady to the right dog, like that lovely sheepdog who graced the birch-tree ladened front yard of the house at the end of the block. We even walked him over to help break the ice. After a traditional sniff-handshake, they dash and dodged around the yard a bit but there were no stars. We brought him back a few times but the relationship never caught fire. Oh well, as dogs will tell you, there are plenty of kibbles in the bag.

Time marched on and though some wonderful prospects virtually fell under his nose, he seemed to show no interest in finding his true love. Yet his innocent amorous advances on our unsuspecting ankles reaffirmed our belief that the desire was there. It just needed to be channelled.

Oh, how we tried. We called sheepdog kennels and clubs and even ran a few ads. Okay its true our intentions were not totally unselfish. I admit we wanted grandchildren and for people who would come to spend our last pennies to patch up his kidneys, you know we would spend as much as we needed to fix his er....love-life.

Alas, all in vain until one day to our great surprise, our giant hair-ball brought his choice home to us. As he introduced her with all of the enthusiasm of a preppie at the prom, we made every effort to make her feel welcome.

"Bingo" by Carly Smith Age 7

Her name was Lilly and she stood proud and very well-kept. Watching the two of them run and frolic was indeed a majestic sight to behold. In her successive visits, we not only grew to accept her as a potential doggie-in-law, we hardly noticed that she was the smallest toy-poodle we had ever seen.

What mattered most was the dizzy joy on Grady's face whenever Lilly came to call; which once again upholds the old motto, "Love is blind" (and oft-times, durable in ways we never imagined).

Yes, love is blind. And I suppose no matter how awkward or painful, love's great triumph is what gives living its spark.

But..ouch!

"Elliot" by Chantel Long Age 10

Hair Mail

All this jabber about how excessively connected people are to their pets and how blinded they are by this love or perhaps by too much fur, I don't know.

What I do know is that every pet-lover insists their pet, no matter how beleaguered-looking to the rest of us, is a real winner. Sure.

Well, all prejudices aside, Grady really was a winner. Now I'm not going to pummel you with platitudes; I have actual-factual proof, on paper.

It all started after a marketing book I had written had brought me a great deal of recognition. That recognition also brought with it a great deal of junk-mail; an endless, relentless trail of high-pressured sales pitches and promises.

On several desperate days, we had to use a metal crowbar to pry the mail from our overstuffed 'country-size' mailbox. Then there was the sifting process through hundreds of pieces just in case their was a legitimate bill or important personal note buried amongst the rubble.

Everyone reaches a boiling-point and one day as I found myself eating up an entire afternoon shoveling through another 'mailstorm', I reached my *maelstrom*.

"Enough!" I screamed, my arm sprained, fingers ravaged with paper-cuts; unable to extract my mail from the box; mail-lock.

I limped inside and with all my remaining strength, groped for the phone. I dialed 911 and asked them to connect me with the Direct Marketing Association (Okay, it was really 411 that I dialed but I didn't want to lose the fervor of the story). The Direct Marketing Association or DMA is the organization who can help you stop most or all of your unwanted junk-mail.

Within three weeks, the mail-flood slowed to a trickle. My arm and hand began to show signs of healing. I was starting to have some time to get my office work done. But as with any time of true bliss, it was short-lived.

It wasn't long before the trickle began to grow into a small stream and everyone knows that junk-mail has the fastest breeding rate know to natologists. Again, I wrote to the DMA, even giving them the names of the latest invaders and again these plumbers of leaky mail did their best. But even the best job becomes ephemeral when it concerns junk-mail. Someone was still breeding my name and I was determined to sniff him out, with the help of the best sniffer around.

For the entire next month, when subscribing to any newsletter or magazine, any time my address was required, I inserted Grady's name in place of my own. Now I could trace the culprit at the source.

This time, I savored another five blissful junk-mail free weeks, with an unstretched functional and happy mailbox. No congratulations that I didn't deserve, no checks that really weren't, no tremendous savings and no giant free prizes. It was a reprieve that allowed me to get back to work in earnest as only the real mail got through; a joyous dream vacation tainted only by the sorry reality that all dreams must end. This time I had my trap set, my net out. This time I was ready.

Grady's first piece of mail, addressed to Grady T. Dawg, was a roll of packing tape (what sheepdog couldn't use that). Then he won a free subscription to a major stock-brokerage letter; then discounts on his next big printing job. Then the floodgates opened once more: grocery coupons, car rebates, an exclusive invitation to receive the American Express Gold-Card, a free bracelet, a piece of genuine polished jade and, of course, the ten-million dollar promise from Ed McMahon.

Was I angry? Not at all. This time I was able to track down the subversive brokers of my address and you better believe the fur flew.

How did Grady feel about his short-lived paper popularity? I think he was hoping for some free sample kibbles. Other than that, I don't think he minded. In fact, I suspect he sensed my gratitude for his efforts.

Got a junk-mail problem? Forward it to your dog; he'll eat it up!

It is said that junk mail...

is only gobbled up by the unwise.

Try telling that to my dog who several times,

has enjoyed sinking his teeth into a

tasty prize!

By Tara Reardon Age 7

Souled

It was way back when, at the ravenous creditor's meeting during my first (and hopefully last) bankruptcy at age 27. As I watched over a million-dollars of my real estate dreams drift away amongst a sea of rabid creditors, my nearest and dearest friend at the time took me to one side and spoke with the soothing reassurance of a reverend out of the old movies. "Don't worry," he said with his charming Texas drawl, "they can't take your soul."
After the hearings, I had plenty of time so I kept thinking about what he said. As I became a stranger to my own banker and wondered if anything would be left, I wondered about this soul that my friend said was definitely mine to keep.

Everyone seems to agree that there is such a thing as a soul but nobody quite knows what it really is. I'm such a realist that I had always believed that once something was gone, it was gone. Then I thought I was being a bit unfair should the souls of any of my dear-departed be trying to reach me.

What is a soul and if it never dies, is it ever born and then does it survive its physical host? Such heavy questions we ponder. Who has the answers? What great theologian, what great sage sits upon a hill with those answers that would satisfy all of us?

Call it low-blood sugar if you like but I was one of those ponderers who kept futilely wrestling with these imponderables, as I asked so many and learned so little. Until I asked my dog.

Obviously, you first have to learn how to speak to a dog which is through his eyes. They were not typical shiny-black dog-eyes. They were far more familiar; humanlike but with greater depth. One was an earthy peaceful-brown, challenged constantly by the other , a reckless, sparkling blue: his Yin and Yang, right on his furry face.

What humans aim for in the cliche-riddled bonding experience is a deep and comfortable eye-contact. The same is true for all animals.

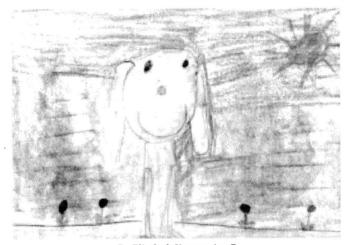

By Elizabeth Kennan Age 7

A gaze into my dog's eyes was not at all a visual experience. It was an adventurous journey, mysterious, deep and winding into worlds much greater than our own; worlds without borders, without limits, without real estate. The eyes are the great winding pathway to that ever-elusive soul and the deeper the journey, the more seasoned the soul.

One of the finest things humans ever did was to admit, in

their theoretical arrogance, that there is this immeasurable thing called a soul. But humans do not like to lend much importance to that which they cannot comprehend. My dog patiently understood and waited. I could see it in his eyes.

Often I think of how much my dog spoke to me through those eyes and how empowering it was to just watch time stop and absorb the experience.

"Chelsea" by Brycen Smith Age 9

Quest for the Wooly Mammoth

You'll never meet a dog with an identity crisis. Each is born knowing their specific job qualifications. As guardians to the death, even a nine-inch Chihuahua becomes in its own mind, a beast far greater than any visitor in question.

The last decade gave us how-to books telling us helpless humans how to do everything except to be ourselves. Many of us became too smart and smug to trust anyone if that advice could not be confirmed by the best authority.

Apparently dogs stayed away from these books because they already knew their jobs. After all, who is better qualified to teach motivation and dedication than a dog. That Chihuahua would attack a wooly mammoth elephant with the intent of killing it and it would die believing itself the victor.

For his first two weeks as our new pet, Grady was largely ornamental. Laying out flat, appearing almost one-dimensional, his rickety legs would rise him upward only with heavy prompting until that stony-still night.

At around 2 a.m., we awakened to his somewhat raspy bark cracking through the darkness. Our half-focused eyes could see the outline of an excessively curious coyote just outside the front door.

"Let me at em, let me at em!" Grady's ready claws dug at the door until it opened, springing 'Grady the Protector' into action.

Of course the coyote easily outran Grady who's still rickety legs were no match for his inflated self-image. After several minutes of some face-saving territorial assertion, he marched proudly back to the house, with an almost clydesdale gait.

By Jack Fitzgerald Age 6

He had proven to us and to himself that he could do his job with unyielding dedication, forever bonded to us as official guardian.

When our two little girls were born, no jealous older sibling was he. Grady was the fine older brother, always there for them. Even in failing health, he would hoist his leaden frame and drag it to wherever the kids were playing and then quickly find the ground, fogging eyes reflecting his peaceful kingdom, which lie just over the horizon. Even while prostrate, he was still standing guard, doing his best; ready to the end for the wooly mammoth.

"Lucky" by David Godinho Age 13

"Max" by John Newton Age 12

The Satellite Dish that Couldn't Receive

Unwary visitors to our home would oft find themselves plowed over by this wildly-roving dish-shaped object. Even those unswerving, ever-dedicated Jehovah's witnesses have, upon seeing it through the tightly-closed storm door, have cried out, "What the Hell is that!" when encountered by the out-of-control satellite dish.

The 'dish' was actually a plastic cone-shaped shroud which prevents an animal from excessive chewing of its legs or back, a habit which Grady could never quite kick. The only clue that this phenomenon was more animal than technological was the almost monstrous bark, augmented by the shape of the cone enshrouding and almost encapsulating the head of this most hairy creature.

This is not another story about flea or tick-infestation or some other skin-condition, mitigated by the use of this odd-shaped plastic cone. This is a story about a dog with no hobbies, no interests, outside of loving and protecting his adoptive family. When he was with his human luminaries, the dish came off and he would either play and walk with us, nuzzle us to death or (his favorite) sleep, switched off like a lamp, alighted only when a hint of simple support was at hand.

He wore the dish for most of his life. Every alternative remedy had been tried to prevent him from chewing himself till there was nothing left but his flapping jaws, longing for more acreage of fur. We knew that no remedy would ever work, not because of what we read in vain in seeking a cure. It was what we read in his face.

Whenever we dared leave the house without him, a Dracula-like force compelled us to catch one-last glimpse of his face. Though we'd fight it, our gaze would be magnetically drawn to both his soulful brown and crazy blue eye. His long, black dog-lips (yes, dogs have them and they're huge) draped limply about his lightly-quivering mouth out of which emanated his famous 'human-whistle'. That was his barely audible shrill that only we could hear.

By Nicole O'Connor Age 8

His message was clear to anyone who understands the nuances of this most powerful of all languages. .."You're leaving me, forever this time. I am abandoned and will never see you again. I shall therefore commit suicide by having one last meal consisting of my own self."

This is why most dogs go into the deepest of mourning every time you leave them behind. When it comes to your departure, be it one minute or eleven days, they don't understand time and they think, "this is it, you're gone, this time you're gone and you're never coming back."

They hedge their bets. They prepare for the worst. They buffer themselves in this perpetual theater of sorrow. Then when your car has disappeared from sight, most shut down and slink into a protective siesta only to spring excitedly to life upon your return, believing that your departure was all just a very bad dream.

No, not from tick nor flea nor summer mange did Grady feel ever-compelled to chew his body. It was out of neurosis, an exacerbation of the departure syndrome. When it came to the usual separation anxiety and resulting nap, this was one animal-satellite dish that just wasn't receiving.

Though his dish was the topic of conversation well beyond Cape Cod, when his image suddenly floats into our subconscious, we see a clean, unfettered sheepdog, fur gloriously pomped, joyously romping through the downy cloud-fields of Heaven, adding the touch of warmth that makes a memory cozy and ever-ingrained.

It is this sense of his purely joyous self which somehow embraces our memories, perhaps through an inexplicable signal transmitted by his torn and tattered satellite dish.

Look kids, there's a star in the sky.
Maybe it's Grady's star.

I know you believe the star shines upon you.

You have to believe or it won't come true.

By Caitlin Cook Age 8

el Thick Skull

Shortly after arriving home with our new and down-and-out adoptive pet, we were confronted with another problem that we couldn't have anticipated in a million years.

The dog could hear. We knew that by his response to surrounding noise. His eyes looked clear. What he could not do was comprehend even the slightest command or request. An initial checkup revealed no concussion nor shock, leaving us with only one last possibility. Grady was retarded.

At first, we thought our new pet was special simply because we rescued him (the poor formerly doomed animal). Suddenly 'special' took on a whole new meaning but being gracious folk who keep a commitment, we still pledged to love and accept our new adoptee.

A retarded Old-English Sheepdog. What more of a challenge could anyone ever imagine? But we pledged to take on our mission in humanity with grace and decorum.

As the weeks passed, Grady grew stronger and happier. So did we as we discovered that the guy was perfectly house-trained; pretty good for an animal otherwise so severely limited. Pretty good for us!

Still something didn't seem right. He always looked at us attentively when we spoke to him. He quickly learned and responded to his name. His eyes were so clear and full of understanding yet that understanding was interrupted somewhere in that brain.

He banged into things occasionally; hit them hard but his skull was as thick and strong as metal. Never even a whimper. Strange. Oh well, you pay $5.00 at a pound for a pet, you take your chances.

Then one sunny afternoon came a startling revelation.

While strolling past a neighbor's lawn, for the first time, Grady's ears perked straight up and off he went as if by robotic-command. When I caught up to him, he was a different dog, delighting in the attention of this group of new-found friends, the neighbor's gardeners. He wobbled his rump and wiggled his stubby little tail so fiercely, I thought his entire back side would fall right off.

As I moved within audible range of this jolly bunch, the mystery unfolded like a clear morning sky.

"Hola, pero, Bien pero. Sientiese. Ah, bien bien pero." Spanish.

A surge of joy raced through my body. Grady was not retarded. He just didn't know English. I watched virtually paralyzed with astonishment as he responded perfectly to every Spanish command. I rushed him home to show my wife who burst into uncontrollable laughter. He wasn't retarded at all. What he was was a Spanish-Old-English Sheepdog.

We savored our new role as tutors and with our Spanish/English Dictionary at hand, we progressed muy rapido with My Fair Doggy. "Caminanos? Walk?"

"Aha" we thought. "Aha, these idiots finally caught on," he must have thought. And over the years, he became fluent in both languages, always preferring his native tongue, mayhaps as a cherished link to his former heartbroken parents somewhere many dusty miles away where he accidentally hopped on a train and suddenly found himself an innocent fugitive, bumping his head on an occasional street lamp, hopelessly groping for a little taco and kibble.

"Shreader" by Paige Titus Age 7

Boing-boing

Grady's death had added a few pounds to both my wife and me. No, it was not emotional eating; it was more locomotional.

His key activity was to coerce one of us into taking him on his daily three-mile winding walk through the nearby forest path. In the 'off' position, Grady lay like a crumpled old throw-rug. A switched-off toy. Closed; only to be activated by the magic words, "Caminanos?" (Spanish for "how about a walk" but you already know that story).

First the ears flickered, followed by the famous glass-shattering whimper. Then up the old boy sprang, pogo-sticking from his back yard roost through the house, hitting a wall or two, accidentally but always stepping on our toes in that grinding way that only big dogs know how to do. Boing, boing, crash! Arruuuf, which was his way of saying "I meant to hit that wall; planned it all along!". Somehow he would bounce out the front door, twirling, biting ("I get excited sometimes") and then he would settle into his peaceful mode as he assumed his forest gait.

You could win a million dollars and still not express the degree of jubilation that this dog expressed daily just for the privilege of taking a simple walk with his beloved.

He never missed a walk, largely due to his uncanny strategic use of either positive reinforcement or guilt. If we put our shoes on at any time within his view, up he'd go, the bouncing mop from here to the nearest wall. It didn't matter if we were on our way to a wedding. Shoes were shoes. Boing, boing. "Let's go."

All those years, we couldn't escape that three-mile obligation and so it became an ingrained part of our own daily rituals. In the heat of summer or at 5-below during a blinding snowstorm. The walk was the law.

Often I would wrap up my over-coffeed, dizzy office days with this sacred return to the quiet of the forest's protective fingers.

I haven't taken that walk, not even once since Grady died.

For now, I am resigned to trade my companion in tranquility for a slightly bigger belly.

"Goldy" by Kaylee Burke Age 7

Another talk with my dog

I find myself
crying out for joy
amidst the shroud of the battering rain

deep surge of cozy warm-chill
vanishes pain.

The ease of a log on the fire
with my dog close at hand,

deep shiny, rainy green...
new again.

What joy I feel
when I can cry

and let the foolish human race
pass me by.

Come on old dog,
creak and stumble with me,
I'll always wait.

Inside they don't realize that
when we walk the other way,

the weather's great.

"Casey" by Allison Thompson Age 7

The Flower Dies

The finest graces in all of us are called upon to cope with endings, especially when explaining them to children. One finds wisdom and peace in the realization that nothing good ever ends well. Otherwise nothing good would ever end.

We knew Grady's days were numbered. His advancing age and recent illness brought him headlong into creaky seniordom. Love had long taken over as his primary pain-soother. He could now only eat the senior diets. 'Senior' was printed right on the dog-food can. It was official and so we made it our mission to give him the best quality of a senior life any loved-one could possibly ask for.

Just the suggestion of being separated from our longtime pal was unbearable as with any dreaded event so we blocked out the lurking reality. Our sweet-old man curled up by our side; a permanent family fixture.

So when the news came one rainy morning, all we felt was great sadness, disappointment, even deep shock. How could he be gone?

I was in front of my computer at the time and began almost unconsciously writing my immediate feelings, like a war correspondent in the midst of battle.

Then I got busy. I found myself cramming my schedule and even tackled some super-draining lawyer headaches that I had put off for ages. To have seen me then, one would never have known that I had just lost such a meaningful friend. My immediate dread was that the kids would arrive home from day-camp in a few hours. I wished I had to do anything but tell the children, especially 5 year-old Ashley. She and Grady were the ever-connected twosome. He cherished her hugs and reserved for her his most special kisses - the full wet-face kind that make children laugh with glee. He was the teddy bear you never dare take away.

I cut my work short to join my wife in picking up the children. On the way, we debated (to say the least) as to how the children would react. We just didn't know where to place all the anger over Grady's rude departure.

We greeted our two little ones with the usual fanfare and then headed towards Grady's favorite beach. Telling children about the loss of any living thing in their lives is such a challenging crash against the protective shell of childhood. Be it a dog, a grandmother or a goldfish, the degree of grief is solely determined by the amount of living love which the young mind must now transfer into a loving memory. Many never come to terms with the concept of separation.

Hand-in-hand, the four of us calmly strolled a little ways along the mildly-crashing waves. I thought about how concerned I was about hurting the children with this sad news. I thought about the constancy of the waves and the ocean as one great loving womb for the old and unfit, giving way to the new; how it always will be. I took a deep breath, sat the family down still holding hands and just let the words come, intending to make this short and sweet.

In story fashion, I spoke about beginnings and endings, how flowers grow and bloom and then wither away. Then Ashley cut in. "But flowers grow back daddy. Suddenly I was lost for words. I didn't want to stifle her own blossoming wisdom. "Yes, new flowers come after the old ones are gone and the old flowers know this."

Then I spoke about the dead animals we sometimes had found in the woods and how we buried them and said good-bye. Perhaps I should have said more. Perhaps I should have created more of a setting or maybe I needed their support as much as they needed mine.

"Ash and Rachie, you gave Grady lots of love and he lived a long and happy life with your love. " My throat was bone dry. I took another breath. "Well, Grady finally got very, very old and....he died."

The three-year-old had just as much heart but was merely too young to comprehend the concept of death. But Ashley crumbled into uncontrollable tears, cutting into our own helpless hearts as we vainly hugged this desperately unhappy little-one. Oh, Grady, you left us with such a burden.

We let her tears bleed hoping they would run dry; our saddened little family so tiny against the crashing shoreline. An eternity later, the sun peaked out, drinking up the fog and Ashley's tears. We knew the coming week would be a tough and lonely one for all of us. We had read no fancy self-help books nor did we consult any specialists. We would help each other through this as a family and in doing so, bond all the more closely. And since most people do not really understand the impact of a lost pet, the experience is generally one exclusively for the family.

Like Grady's funeral. This is a very important and definite aspect of saying good-bye to any beloved pet. It prevents the children from nurturing false hopes and wondering where he may have gone.

The funeral was precious. We each said our peace and our good-byes. "We will always love you Grady", Ashley spoke so musically after which she and Rachel placed little drawings they made at his grave and then helped fill in the final shovel-fulls of dirt.

Yes the world is full of cycles and statistics and the old makes way for the new but we were still angry and wounded. We wished this special flower could have shined upward and spectacular for just one moment longer.

The flower does all it can do and then its time comes. The family committed to healing does indeed heal.

"Mickey" by Jillian Temple Age 7

Now I know

Grady was obnoxiously affectionate, like those elderly aunts who attempt to suffocate you with either an excessive hug or via the deadly chemical warfare of excessive perfume.

You had to push Grady away to get him to cease his endless kissing and nuzzling. It would shock the unanointed to learn what a powerful acquaintance device a dog's nose can be. Seasoned dog-parents will uphold the fact that no territory is sacred from this well-meaning *cannus proboscis.*

Even still, after all this time, I expect to misspell a word as his ever-dangerous nose would suddenly sneak up under my elbow and send my typing arm bouncing all over the keyboard. Though he always meant it as a loving gesture, it also gave me a badly needed excuse for occasional and inexplicable letter combinations.

He was there, always there and I suppose we get comfortably spoiled by the constancy of love. In its sudden absence, we are furious at the moon, at the wind, the living and still loving and most especially, at the dead. It doesn't matter why they left us. Every reason is unfair and wrong. The anger boils and finally cools and then we're either confused or we begin to ask the right questions.

As I get over the shock of the loss of this dear buddy and find no new home for the love especially reserved for Grady, I find myself asking the one comforting question:

not why did he have to die but instead, what more could I have asked of him! All he ever did was foster love and laughter.

While his love could only grow and encourage more life, his body was old, tired and pushed to its limits. He was an endless bestower of love but quite aloof about receiving it. It was as if he was saying, "I can't let you get too friendly with me because that would make my departure all the more painful."

He knew.

"Katie" by Suzanne Davis Age 9

Psychic Sidekick

I write my books to pay my debts
to those who loved me

and somewhere I know
Grady's up above me..

looking down, saying...

"I know life is hard right now.

Business is tough and you can't run with me in the
wood when the world tries to tell you all those stupid
'shouldn'ts & shoulds.'

But I'm watching,
you know I am
and you must know that I still can.

Those business headaches,
you will fix 'em
those other doubts...you're gonna nix 'em.

And that impossible dream of a little one?
The child will come to you and mom.
It's here with me now and it wants to be born
but you have to help it through a very tough storm.

So if you live to well past 80...
Remember me, your old pal Grady.

Somewhere past life I speak to you.
You saved my life once,
and I pay my debts too!"

"Rixie" by Julie Johnson Age 9

"Spotty" by Dawn Curry Age 8

The Gardener

Without love, a pet could arguably be the greatest financial liability a family could ever have.

As with any dedicated dog-lover, we saw Grady as the most loving dog on the continent. But in his last few months, Grady was also incontinent, unable, or just too tired to distinguish our outside lawn from our brand-new stain-resistant livingroom carpet. Or maybe advancing age made him excessively territorial and he was just doing his job (and keeping carpet-installers employed) while proving that when a dog becomes as sick as a dog, there really is no such thing as a stain-resistant carpet.

But our love for this well-intentioned furry fellow was unstainable and superseded our highest levels of aggravation; especially concerning his last winter, when in a few short days, he went from a bouncing old, well-meaning 'pup' to a very hurting old man who suddenly behaved as if his bloodstream was now comprised of peanut-butter.

Suddenly, one frigid Sunday, every (and I mean 'every') organ in his body simply went on strike and something told me his rapid deterioration called for immediate action. I half-carried him to the car and rushed to our favorite vet who Grady had already been keeping quite busy.

My mind was pre-programmed to believe that this exceptionally talented doctor would quickly identify some invading germ, prescribe the perfect magic bullet and the old boy would be all back together. The doctor gave us the pills; a little bigger dosage than usual, plus a prelimi-nary diagnosis: either Lyme Disease or some related curse from the wild. Home we went, assuring Grady he would feel better within a day. For a day, he did improve a bit and even tried eating a little thereby calming his worried parents.

Hopes and the clean carpet soon faded on the following day when he could scarcely move anything except his bowels. "My God, how our love is tested sometimes," I thought as my wife and I left him at the vet the next morn-ing for what we thought would be just a little more oc-tane in that magic bullet.

Home again, our incontinent dog left in competent hands, it suddenly occurred to me that this worried parent hadn't slept more than a few hours during the past few days. I closed my office at 3:00 that day and went straight to bed for a well-deserved power-nap. Just as the pure ecstasy of desperately needed sleep was taking hold, the phone rang. Half-asleep, I faded deeper knowing that my wife would barricade me from all calls unless...

As I heard her hurried footsteps, I immediately reached for the phone. By the time she opened the door, I had heard the worst of all news. "It's his kidneys. I don't think he's gonna make it," our vet said.

Within that split-second, I committed myself to employ-ing every possible resource, every technological advance-ment, every last penny we had, and more to save the dog whose unconditional love had so many times saved me. He would live and everything and everyone blocking this

"Grady" by Ashley Bronson Age 8

effort was but a barrier to be negotiated around or crashed through.

Within ten minutes, we had located one of the finest veterinary centers in the country: the Tufts New England Medical Center in Grafton, Massachusetts. While I was fully prepared to fly him anywhere, or even to rent a dialysis machine, the Tufts Hospital was just a two-hour drive. By good fortune and via the compassion and dedication of so many fine animal lovers before me; this miracle center of last resort stood ready to provide the best and most advanced lifesaving technology. No better medical care exists, even for humans.

It was to this faint spark of hope we rocketed; just Grady and me. He lay across my lap in my just-reupholstered sedan. As he moaned and cried in between getting sick on my lap and car, I kept stroking his back; feeling him twitch occasionally in pain even to my gentlest touch but knowing he needed that reassuring contact. Still I had to talk to him this way so that he might survive this rescue voyage and perhaps fight even his own desire to just give up and melt away.

I suppose this may be a time when owners of clearly fading animals think more of their need to be loved than to respect the reality of an animal's fate but I wouldn't let him die. "No", I kept screaming against the impenetrable stoniness of the black stormy night. "No" to the hiding stars like thunder to the heavens. "You cannot take him."

Then I'd beg, "Please don't take him", I cried softly into the merciless frigid night, "please, oh please."

By 7:00 that evening, we had arrived in record-time at the country-nestled medical complex. Grady was barely alive; his dry tongue hung lamely, his eyes, waxen and begging for permanent relief, crying to fade into the tranquility of death's embrace. He could no longer walk and didn't even squirm as I hoisted his seventy-five pound frame in my arms as if he were a sleeping lamb.

Once in the doors, the best of what human beings are, took over. That which makes humans humane; that artful blend of love, dedication and ultimate technology. I could only liken that moment to the feeling I had right before the birth of my children; whereby all is taken over by the onrushing swoon of faith; the knowledge that miracles that shouldn't happen, were going to happen.

Before Grady's full medical evaluation, an even more dire medical emergency arrived: a German Shepherd, also in kidney failure but able to walk into the examining room under her own power. In what seemed like moments, a tearful family emerged from the room. Their dog was dead. What chance would Grady have?

The team surrounded Grady as my embattled heart refused to accept the bleak chances of his survival and refused to be filled with anything but the awesome power of hope.

His creatinine (the toxicity level in his kidneys) was well above 12, which generally indicates total renal failure. His liver was distended and his heart was beginning to beat irregularly. The doctors were crystal-clear about his bleak prognosis: hour-to-hour.

Within moments of my signing my pledge to cover any and all lifesaving attempts, he was whisked away and placed on a continuous i.v. solution in the hopes that it might flush out the toxins. Massive doses of Penicillin were also introduced to kill the suspected invader (either Lyme Disease or Lepto-Spirosis). There was still the other irreversible possibility that his time was done and that old age was taking its final curtain (the suddenness of it all precluded my accepting this final theory).

My love and hope were blindingly tough and unswerving. My last gesture before leaving Grady to the fate of the intensive care facilities was to take his head firmly in my hand, look deeply into his eyes and then I softly gave him the sternest, most challenging reprimand of his life: "You fight hard," I spoke with all the reassurance I could muster. "You work with these people to get well. Now promise me!" I was doing my best Oral Roberts until I felt certain the message got through.

There were small blizzards for the next several days. I was staying nearby to spend a little time with him each day and to preach to him. For the first few days, there was little change and there was more heart trouble and he would not eat at all but at least there were still days. My visits were short. Upon my arrival, they would disconnect the i.v. tubes to his legs, unplug the monitor for his heart and hand this poor animal to me. To accommodate the wires and plugs, his legs were half-shaved and his chest was also bare. It was amusing to think that part his medical therapy would temporarily transform him into a Poodle.

During our 15 or 20 minute tube and wire break, I would take him out in the snow and we would walk 10 or 15 yards. I would talk to him and encourage him to continue. After several days, there were signs of slight improvement although he still wasn't eating and the doctors were running out of veins in which to introduce the i.v. needles. On the following Saturday, we brought our children into the hospital to celebrate his fourteenth birthday (a few weeks early) with his favorite chocolate cake. When he couldn't even take a bite, we knew he was still far away from any real recovery.

A few days later, he took a few swallows of chicken soup, then a few more. And a few days after that, the doctor called to give us a release date. I methodically wrote it down, then hung up the phone and then my wife and I wept for joy.

On his real birthday, we brought him home, weak but alive and still requiring a daily i.v. solution, an activity which became part of our routine.

Anything to keep him with us, old but not ailing; grateful that we did not have to make that tough but sometimes wholly unselfish decision to end pure agony and put him to sleep.

We were grateful that he had returned to ruin the carpets, as much as he wanted. The arrival of spring saw Grady recovered, and content to enjoy his final months as a peaceful, healthy old-timer, full of love and an obvious sense of being loved.

People have asked us if saving his life was worth the $3,200 during a time when we had so many other debts. More specifically, many people thought we were just plain out of our heads to spend that kind of money just to have given our dog a little extra time. And some insisted that we just should have put him to sleep when the suffering first started.

I will never understand how people can poison their gardens and then expect flowers to grow as if nothing has changed.

"Dot" by Corinne Silva Age 7

Deepest Symphonies

The great joy of expressing one's feelings in writing is that others can share, relate, support, ridicule and ultimately teach. My writing has helped me to grow by allowing me to discover how so many people can share similar (though highly private) feelings.

When Grady's kidneys first went critical, I remembered certain popular songs that were playing on the radio at the time. To this day, hearing those songs takes me right back to that frightening moment when I first carried my dying old dog to the car on that dark snowy night.

Pain overwhelmed his ragged body to the point where just touching him caused him to wince and twitch. As I left him at Tufts, I wondered if he understood any of my words of support or if he felt he was being punished for something. It's a kind of empathy that only a pet-lover can understand.

Two days later, the oddest sensation awakened me. The pain around my lower back and kidneys was so acute, I could scarcely get out of bed. "Oh my God," I thought, " did I catch what Grady had? No, it couldn't be." I forced myself to take a good walk followed by the hottest shower I could stand and then headed to the animal hospital to be with my struggling companion.

Just to know he was still alive was cause for joy. I spent as much time as they would allow him off his intravenous needles and heart monitor. I talked to him and encouraged him. I felt no pain.

That evening as I left the hospital the pain returned as if a demon reawakening. It's depth and unfamiliarity frightened me. It was snowing again and I was haunted by a song that was playing on the radio all that week. I headed straight for bed, hoping my body was sufficiently tired to sleep through the pain.

In the morning, the pain was so severe, every motion hurt. I tried the walk-and-shower routine and drank some extra coffee to anesthetize the pain and made it to Grady. This time my visit did not distract me from my own pain and I knew I had better get some help.

At around ten that evening, I found myself sitting anxiously in a dirty hospital waiting room. What seemed like hours later, a physician's assistant finally tended to me. They ran blood tests and did a very thorough checkover.

They found nothing, no indication of any illness and suggested that I might be under a great deal of stress. This is their polite way of suggesting that I could be imagining the ordeal.

As hypochondriacal as it sounds, I was still in a great deal of pain as I left the emergency room, though I wondered if this was my psyche's way of sympathizing with a loved-one. With the power of that knowledge and a good night's rest, I began to feel better. So did Grady. A week later, the pain went away altogether and as the snowstorms began quieting and the fog of the crisis lifted, the reality came into focus. In lifting and carrying my squirming 75-pound dog all over the place, I had sprained my back.

The other day, that song played on the radio again and I felt okay.

I Carried You
..when your own legs wouldn't do,
hard as they tried.

You felt so ashamed
but you were not to blame because You Carried Me
when my father died.

"Bingo" by Kyle Hatherlen Age 6

I'm Here

This was a decent, well-meaning dog but let's get real; every animal has at least a few annoying faults.

For an eternity, our station-wagon made a squeaky noise. We'd bring it to the shop where knowledgeable technicians would exact minor repairs. After much verbal reassurance and a slightly annoying bill, we'd drive away only to return a short time later, still squeaking.

Back and forth to the knowledgeable technicians who exacted more exact repairs: the fan-belt, brakes, the axle. Squeak, squeak. More bills. We tolerated it because we are people of faith who believe that one day modern science would find a cure for our mystery squeak. But even when that great day came, there was still a squeak which we all hear to this day.

Whenever we put Grady in the back of the car, he began this breathy, high-pitched pulsation - a constant symphonic anathema that scratched at our brains and immediately induced minor headaches.

Nothing could stop him, nothing except time. Once we were five minutes from the house, he would cease his destructive attack and then lay down.

In those five minutes, he had finished saying, "Hey we're going somewhere!"

This was followed by a peaceful drive to about five minutes from anywhere; sleeping kids and dog, chatting mom and dad finally getting a chance to catch up with each other until...as if triggered by the slowing down of the car, our Old English Sheep Beacon would resume his killer squeaks as if a warning radar.

Eventually, modern science prevailed and our car's squeak was arrested, but Grady maintained his squeak to his dying day. When we ate he did it, when we put our shoes on he did it. Still I don't think he meant to annoy us. After all it wasn't his fault that our ear drums weren't designed well.

"Kessy" by Jenna Schermerhorn Age 8

Besides, this is what love is all about...tolerance, unconditional acceptance, give or take a few squeaks here and there because animals and people often have funny ways of saying, "I'm here."

We're goin' somewhere, I don't care where.
I'm here
I'm here.

For a run at the beach or a look at the moon,
I'm just so glad
to be with you.

To the hardware store to buy some string,
I don't care,
you've taken me.

By Ashley Bronson Age 8

Go Lie Down

While you could fill a book with the many ways in which a dog proceeds to lay himself down, I wouldn't print too many copies.

Lying down for a dog is not merely a function, it is a ritual, perhaps either inherited or taught to them by superstitious ancestors who most likely spent their lives on a merry-go-round.

Next time before you go to bed, stand on the mattress and try spinning around ten or twenty times as if a screw, winding down to nowhere. Does it make sleep more palatable? What happens?

Everyday as our dog became this furry-go-round, we wondered why with about the same fervor as one might wonder why air exists? In other words the knowledge would not change anything.

As friends witnessed Grady's 'spin-cycle', over the years, they would assert various theories. Here are the five main ones:

1) The softening theory- These observers attributed the behavior to a dog's instinctive habit of trampling the ground to make a softer bed for himself before sleeping. Except for the fact that trampling usually makes the ground harder, this isn't such a bad thought.

2) The eviction theory- purported that in the wild, dogs used to spin around to chase away unwanted rodents and

other pests. Nothing here about what a sleeping dog does if those evicted beasties return during the night.

3) The lighthouse theory- This group, headed by a physicist, maintained that a dog likes to take take several scouting looks around to make sure the world is safe around him (See theory 2).

4) There were the 'dizzy theorists' who held that dogs cannot fall asleep unless they render themselves into a near-nauseating dizziness (we all know what a pleasure it is to sleep with an ever-fluctuating horizon).

"Ben" by Pamela Gill Age 10

5) Still an astronomer offered this additional assertion; dogs always spin clockwise in accordance with the spin of the earth. Now there's some information that should improve anyone's standard of living. Until right in front

of this great scientific mind, Grady stopped, looked around as if to say, "now where was I", and then began spinning counterclockwise. I believe that astronomer is now a short-order cook at the diner just outside of town.

So honored we were to receive such a wealth of invaluable and irrefutable scientific data and all for free. What did we believe, you may be wondering with bated breath as you join us in this the most perplexing of all worldly phenomena. First, as his parents, we believe that we knew him better than even the greatest scientific minds.

For our explanation, we have to go back to when he was a much younger circler. He would spin once or twice and down he went. No fanfare, no long drawn-out procession until he noticed us watching him. Suddenly there was an extra rotation. A few days later, another, and then more every time we watched.

If he thought we weren't watching, he would go straight down but as soon as our eyes were trained upon him, he began his cycle. We theorized that if he had lived another two and one-half years, he would never lie down but instead, spin the entire evening away.

Or maybe this was the way a dog stirs the soul.

Yes, it was yet another test of our patience and it was starting to eat into our time but without cable TV in our town, we were kind of a captive audience, perhaps hypnotized by the constant spinning.

Still he was nice to have around.

"Bingo" by Brittany Lonergan Age 6

Your Shadow Dog

Even in the faintest light,
there's a shadow in the night
making everything alright
keeping you from cold and fright.

Round the corner lurks my fuzzle
lookin' for a place to nuzzle

(sayin') "okay if I cuddle near?
I'll lend you a floppy ear.
I can? Oh good, I heard you tell me.
I'll dart my nose into your belly
up and down and left and right
Ahhh, there's your heart. Now that's just
right!"

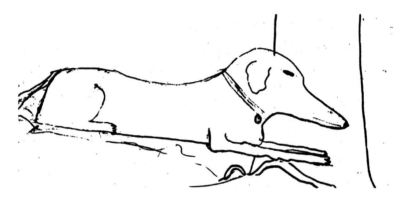

"Howie" by Ian Roberts Age 10

A Sheepdog's Final Farewell

I have to leave.
Don't mourn or grieve.

I've done all the crying for both of us;
that, you must believe!

My tears are the fount
of some lost puppy,
some lost and battered animal

still praying

for a second chance to love
and be loved.

My love stays with you
as I leave the living shore

Go on, take it all.
In death, I don't need it anymore.

A hearty welcome for my final sleep.
I am tired and can no longer tend my sheep.

"Nicky" by Christopher Boulay Age 10

Again?

It was all so disconcerting when an employee showed me an ad for sheepdog puppies. Only six months had passed since Grady died and I wasn't ready to just replace him. Besides, I had just finished cleaning the carpet.

I greeted the entire prospect of a new pet with that sleepy enthusiasm we humans reserve for those moments when we don't know how to say no. My kids, wife and my feet said, "at least go and look and the little fur-devils."

I think I set a record for the number of times one can say, "we are not getting a puppy" within a fifteen-minute car ride. As soon as we pulled in their driveway, I could already smell that smell made by puppies much too young to know any better; In fact I could smell all seven of them. The smell told me one thing for certain, that the sellers would be highly motivated.

My little four and five-year old daughters seemed oblivious to the piercing puppy odor against which deodorizers had little effect. This made me realize why kids and puppies get along so well. These puppies would have to be incredibly cute so as to make even a dysfunctional nostril forget what was assailing it.

The kids fell in love with all seven. My wife fell in love with all seven plus the parents. The weighty prospect of my house full of puppies and their parents crushed my spirits with a leaden force. And of getting new carpeting again so soon. Most of all, I was envisioning Grady's ghost; his bewildering eyes beckoning, "How could you betray me?"

I couldn't. We politely thanked the tired owners and left with no promises. As I drove home and wondered if I could ever get my brain to forget that puppy smell to the seventh power, I began to sort things out. Looking at the hope in the eyes of my family, I realized that people who mourn the loss of a pet or any loved-one are the most selfish people in the universe, especially a mourning father of two sweet and innocent children.

They deserved the love that only a puppy can give. Two days later when we went back and picked out our new puppy, I noticed that it didn't smell as bad this time.

It's now been a while since our Teddy (Sir Teddy Bear of Bronson, to be exact) has become a integral part of our family. As with most correct decisions, the correctness of this one spoke for itself.

Sir Teddy, the fifth sheepdog to enter my life, has reinvented my enthusiasm and okay, our search for yet another new carpet.

Once Too

When your pet dies
you're deeply blue

you wonder what
you'll ever do.

Then puppy comes
and kisses you

and old dog ghosts
dreamt up by you

say, "Go ahead
begin anew

cause all of us
were young once too!"

Dear reader,

The staff of Bestsell Publications join Mr. Bronson in thanking you for reading <u>Dog-Gone</u>. We hope you have found it helpful. The purchase of this book helps support a small, homespun American company dedicated to producing these high quality print, audio and video materials.

Our other books currently available are:

Early Winter   (Learning to live, love and laugh again after any painful loss)
 by Howard Bronson
ISBN 0-9616807-2-5

A Winter's Passage, the Early Winter Sequel
(A Decade of Growing Beyond Grief in Today's Independent Adult Family)
by Howard Bronson
ISBN 0-9616807-4-1

Great Idea! Now What?:(A Friendly Guide for Bringing your Idea, Dream, Invention or Business From Birth to Bonanza for Even Less Than a Little Money)
By Howard Bronson
ISBN 0-9616807-0-9

The above three books and <u>Dog Gone</u> may be obtained in three different ways:
1) You may go to your local bookstore and if they do not have the title in stock, they will order it for you. 2) You may call our toll-free number at 1-800-247-6553. 3) You may send a check directly to our company, using the following discount schedule: For <u>Early Winter</u>, <u>Winter's Passage</u>, and <u>Great Idea! Now What?</u>, the price is the same:

NOTE: ALL PRICE LISTS APPLY ONLY WHEN SENDING CHECK DIRECTLY TO BESTSELL PUBLICATIONS

Quantity	Cost	Shipping	Total
One Book	$ 8.00	$2.00	$10.00
Two Books	$15.00	$3.00	$18.00
Three Books	$20.00	$3.00	$23.00
Four Books	$22.50	$4.00	$26.50
Five Books	$25.00	$5.00	$30.00
Six to Ten Books	$ 4.50 each	$ .65 per book	
Eleven to Fifty Books	$ 4.00 each	$ .35 per book	

Please use order form on facing page

Price Schedule for **Dog Gone**   by Howard Bronson   ISBN 0-9616807-8-4

Quantity	Cost	Shipping	Total	
One Book	$ 9.95	$2.00	$11.95	
Two Books	$18.95	$3.00	$21.95	
Three Books	$28.95	$3.00	$31.95	Special Discounts are available for FundraisingPrograms.
Four to Ten Books	$ 9.00 each	$ .75 per book		Please write Bestsell for details.
Eleven to Fifty Books	$ 8.00 each	$ .50 per book		

Price Schedule for the **Through the Seasons** Bereavement Cassette Tape

This is a 90-minute tape dealing with every aspect of bereavement and recovery. This uplifting, information-packed tape features Howard Bronson and bereavement specialist Dr. Frank Clouse. It also includes some original music and poetry.

Quantity	Cost	Shipping	Total
One Tape	$14.95	$2.00	$16.95
Two Tapes	$24.95	$3.00	$27.95
Three Tapes	$27.95	$3.00	$30.95
Four to Ten Tapes	$ 8.00 each	$ .75 per tape	
Five to Fifty Tapes	$ 5.00 each	$ .35 per tape	

ORDER FORM

Make all checks payable to: Bestsell Publications • 6 Samba Circle • Sandwich, MA 02563

TITLE	QUANTITY	COST including Shipping
Early Winter		
A Winter's Passage		
Great Idea! Now What?		
Dog Gone		
Through the Seasons audio tape		

Sub Total _____

5% Mass Tax (Residents Only) _____   **Total** _____

Name _____

Street _____

City _____

State _____ Zip _____